SING OUT, IRENE

JAMES MARSHALL

HOUGHTON MIFFLIN COMPANY BOSTON

FOR
HARRIET HERSCHEL
AND
JOHN McFARLAND
WITH
LOVE

One afternoon in spring, Irene came home from school with tears in her eyes.

She went straight to her room, without touching her milk and cookies.

"Dear, oh dear," said her mother, Sophie, "I think Irene is unhappy about something."

Sophie peeked into Irene's room.

"Irene," she said softly, "why are you hiding under the bed?"

Irene didn't answer.

"This is serious," said her mother.

"Something must have happened at school," thought Sophie. "I think I'll pay a visit to Irene's teacher."

Irene's teacher, Miss Jones, couldn't have been nicer.

"Poor Irene is unhappy because I asked her to play the part of the Toadstool in the Spring Pageant."

"Oh," said Sophie.

When Sophie got home she made Irene a peanut
butter and jelly sandwich, and they sat down
for a long chat.

"Sometimes we have to do things we don't like,"
Sophie said. "Just do the best you can, and I'll
be so proud of you."

Irene felt better.

She went outside to play on her skateboard.

Soon she forgot all about the Spring
Pageant — until she skated by her friends
Bridget, Brian, and Bruce!
"There goes Irene the Toadstool!" they
called out.
Irene's feelings were hurt.

A moment later Irene crossed paths with
Junior Ditswater.

"Where are you going, Irene?" he shouted.

"Looking for toadstools?"

Irene decided to go home.

She sat in the yard swing, thinking.

Sophie looked out the kitchen window.

"I hope Irene isn't brooding," she thought.

Irene had made her decision. She would do her best. Every night after dinner she practiced her number with her mother.

The Spring Pageant was a huge success.
But very few of the performers stood out.
Mrs. Ditswater complained that she could
not locate Junior in the dance of the
April Posies.

Only Irene was special. She was the only toadstool in the whole pageant.

When the performance was over, all the
players crowded around Irene.

They were green with envy.

Sophie was so proud. So was Miss Jones.

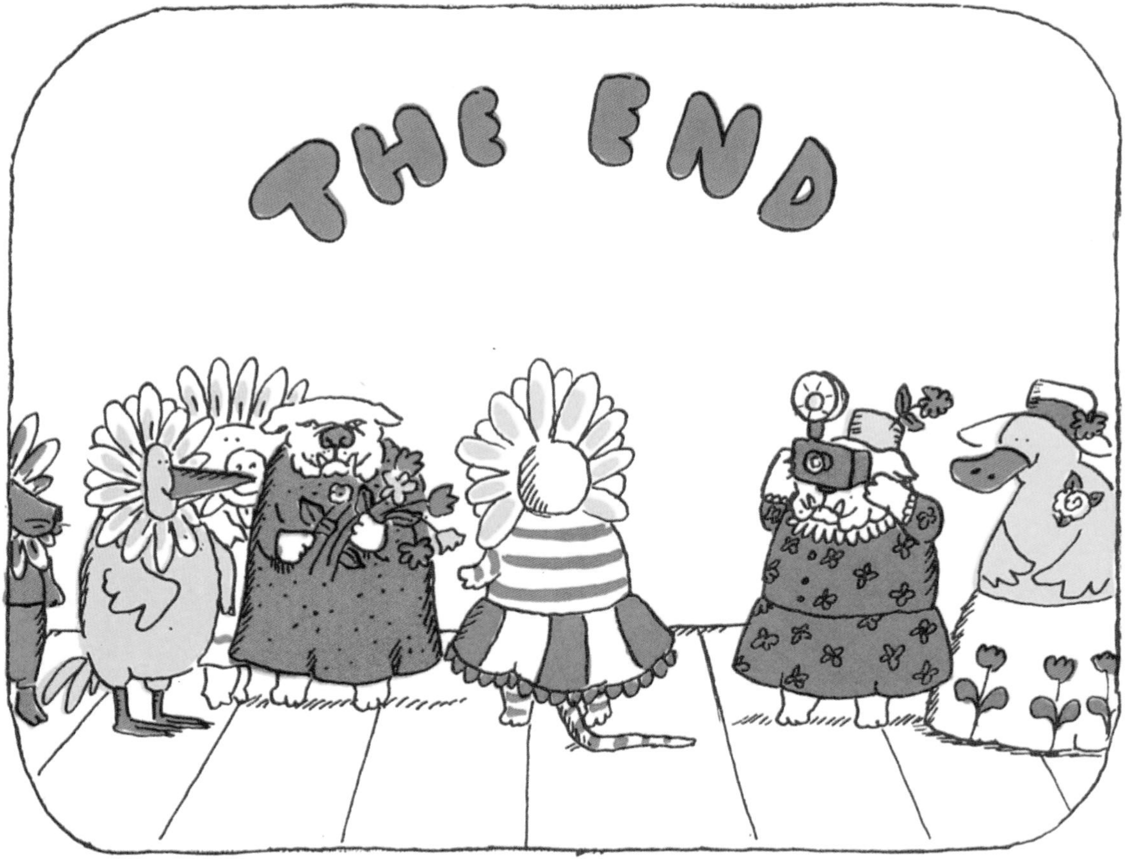
THE END

James Marshall, the creator of many hilarious books for children, including *Miss Nelson Is Missing* and *The Stupids Step Out,* has no rival when it comes to goofy fun. Filled with the same silly spirit and charm, his *Four Little Troubles* provide cozy comfort to young readers facing the universal troubles of childhood.

The *Four Little Troubles* series includes:
Eugene
Sing Out, Irene
Snake: His Story
Someone Is Talking about Hortense, written by Laurette Murdock

Reptar to the Rescue!

By Stephanie St. Pierre
Illustrated by George Ulrich

SCHOLASTIC INC.
New York Toronto London Auckland Sydney

Based on the TV series RUGRATS® created by Klasky/Csupo Inc.
and Paul Germain as seen on NICKELODEON®

ISBN 0-590-18989-1

12 11 10 9 8 7 6 5 4 3 2 1   7 8 9/9 0 1 2/0

Printed in the U.S.A.
First Scholastic printing, October 1997